did I tell you I Love YOU today?

by **Deloris Jordan**

with **Roslyn M. Jordan**

illustrated by **Shane W. Evans**

Simon & Schuster Books for Young Readers

NEW YORK   LONDON   TORONTO   SYDNEY

SIMON & SCHUSTER BOOKS FOR YOUNG READERS
An imprint of Simon & Schuster Children's Publishing Division
1230 Avenue of the Americas, New York, New York 10020
Text copyright © 2004 by Deloris Jordan and Roslyn M. Jordan
Illustrations copyright © 2004 by Shane W. Evans
SIMON & SCHUSTER BOOKS FOR YOUNG READERS is a trademark of Simon & Schuster, Inc.
Book design by Dan Potash
The text for this book is set in Mrs. Eaves.
The illustrations for this book are rendered in oil.
Manufactured in the United States of America
2 4 6 8 10 9 7 5 3 1
Library of Congress Cataloging-in-Publication Data
Jordan, Deloris. Did I tell you I love you today? / Deloris Jordan and Roslyn M. Jordan ;
illustrated by Shane W. Evans.—1st ed. p. cm. Summary: A mother describes the many
ways that she shows her love for her child throughout the day. ISBN 0-689-85271-1
[1. Mother and child—Fiction. 2. Love—Fiction. 3. Day—Fiction. 4. Stories in rhyme.]
I. Jordan, Roslyn M. II. Evans, Shane W., ill. III. Title.
PZ8.3.J7647 Di 2004 • [E]—dc22 • 2003010778

A Note from the Author

Love is every bit as important a human need as food, clothing, or shelter because it's one of the early experiences that determine how we view ourselves and relate to others. It is important to say that we love our children, but it is even more important to make them feel loved.

Whenever I tucked my children into bed at night, I was saying "I love you" by my actions. When I drove them to school, met with their teachers, or even disciplined them, I was saying "I love you." Every day I would tell them "I love you" in so many ways, and it is my wish that *Did I Tell You I Love You Today?* will help children to understand and see the many ways parents show their love, time after time.

Delores Jordan

As the sun slowly rises and the moon fades away,
while you are still sleeping, I sit quietly and pray.

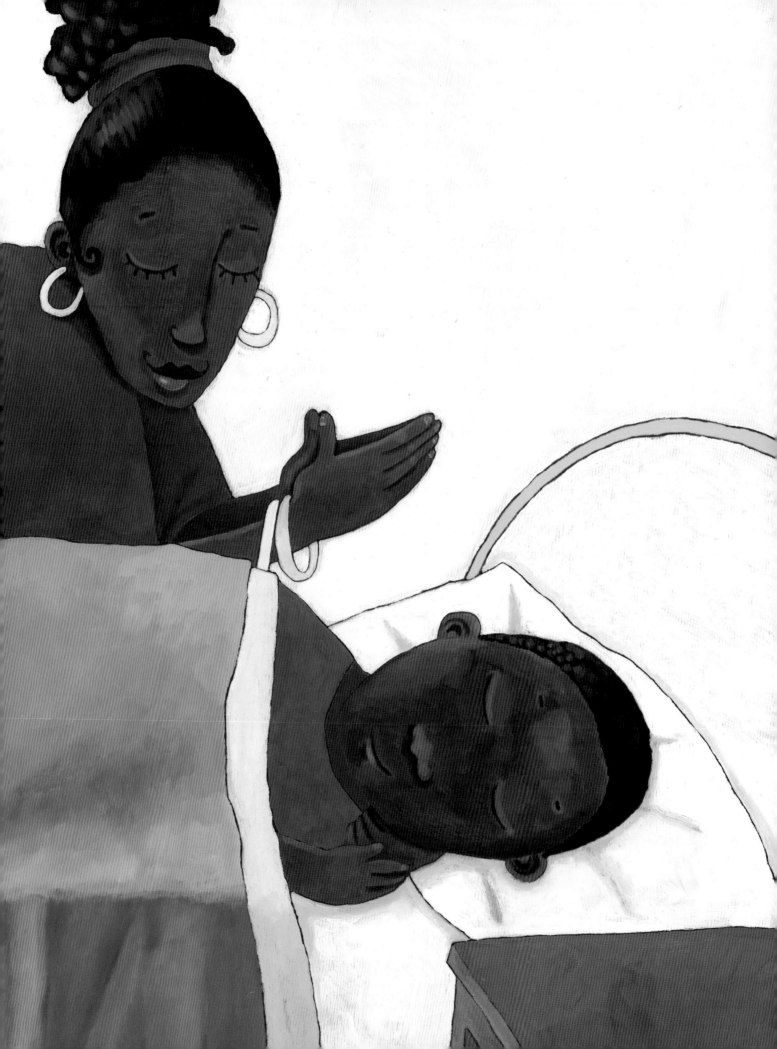

Remembering our time together and the things you like to do,
I'm thinking of ways I can help to bring out the best in you.
Searching for ways to encourage you in all I do and say,
I pray for ways to tell you best that "I love you" today.

When I am done and you awake, I make sure I am there
to clean you up and get you dressed, to brush and comb your hair.

Helping you look and feel your best is one important way
I take the time to tell you, child, that "I love you" today.

Next we play our favorite game of
clean the room and make the bed.
Then I fix your breakfast and
make sure that you are fed.

Keeping you healthy, well, and strong, that is another way
I take the time to tell you, child, that "I love you" today.

Now it's off to school for you, where learning is made fun.
With teachers and friends you spend the day until my work is done.

Making sure you learn and grow is yet another way
I take the time to tell you, child, that "I love you" today.

After school and work are done
and we're on our way home,
we stop sometimes at our favorite place
to spend special time alone.
Taking time for only you is yet another way
I take the time to tell you, child, that "I love you" today.

Bursting with excitement, you have so much to say
as you take me step by step through all you learned today.
Taking time to listen to you is yet another way
I take the time to tell you, child, that "I love you" today.

When dinner is through and you're ready for bed,
we find our own cozy nook.
I draw you close and hold you tight
and read your favorite book.
Making you feel protected and safe is the most important way
I take the time to tell you, child, that "I love you" today.

Late in the night,
when the moon is shining against the dark so deep,
when the world has grown silent and still,
and you are fast asleep . . .

when the stars are twinkling in the sky,
each one burning bright,
and your sweet, innocent face is all aglow,
beneath the heaven's light . . .

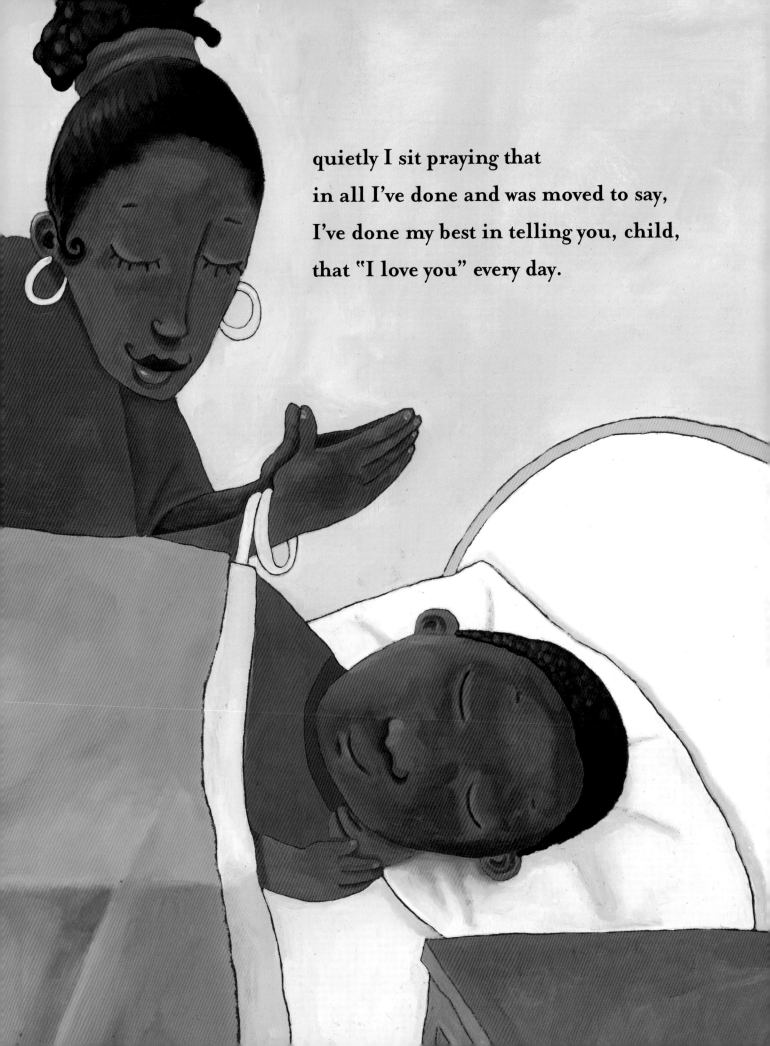

quietly I sit praying that
in all I've done and was moved to say,
I've done my best in telling you, child,
that "I love you" every day.

I dedicate this book to all of the parents of the world, for I acknowledge your commitment. I know a mother's love for her child is greater than any obstacle. From childhood to adulthood you can see the unending power of a mother's love. To my adult children and to my grandchildren, for all the cards you have made to share your love with me. Each one is so very special. I love you.—Grandma (D. J.)

This book is dedicated to my Heavenly Father, who continues to lavish His unfailing love, enduring mercy, and abundant grace on me. To my mom, who has given so much more than any child could ask.—R. M. J.

Thank you, God. Dedicated to the funniest little brother, Bobby J. Love you!—S. W. E.

Thanks to my publisher, Simon & Schuster Children's Division, and to the editors who contributed to making this book happen. To Amy Berkower, I would like to express gratitude to you for your encouragement and assistance.—D. J.

Thanks to Simon & Schuster for this blessed opportunity and to my mother, who has continued to encourage me in life no matter what.—R. M. J.